About the Author

Award-winning author Heather Peck has enjoyed a varied life. She has been both farmer and agricultural policy adviser, volunteer covid vaccinator and NHS Trust Chair. She bred sheep and alpacas, reared calves, broke ploughs, represented the UK in international negotiations, specialised in emergency response from Chernobyl to bird flu, managed controls over pesticides and GM crops, saw legislation through Parliament and got paid to eat Kit Kats while on secondment to Nestle Rowntree.

She lives in Norfolk with her partner Gary, two dogs, two cats, two hens and a female rabbit named Hero.

Also by Heather Peck

THE DCI GELDARD NORFOLK MYSTERIES

Secret Places
Glass Arrows *
Fires of Hate **
The Temenos Remains **
Dig Two Graves **
Beyond Closed Doors
Death on the Rhine (novella)**
Death on the Norwich Express (novella)

Milestones (thriller)***

*shortlisted for the East Anglian Book Award
prize for fiction 2021
**Firebird Book Award Winner
***Page Turner Book Awards 2024 best crime novel

EXPEDITION TO DEATH

BOOKS FOR CHILDREN

Tails of Two Spaniels **
The Animals of White Cows Farm
The Pixie and the Bear

**Firebird Book Award Winner

Published in 2025 by Ormesby Publishing

Ormesby St Margaret

Norfolk

www.ormesbypublishing.co.uk

Author photograph by John Thompson 2021

British Library Cataloguing in Publication Data

A CIP catalogue record for this book is available from the British Library.

Page design and typesetting by Ormesby Publishing

Expedition to Death

Heather Peck

Ormesby Publishing

Acknowledgments

My thanks to Gary for everything

and many thanks yet again to my beta readers Geoff Dodgson, Alison Tayler and Gary Westlake for their constructive criticism and comments.
This book is all the better for your help.

Thanks also to Sharon Gray at CluedUpEditing for her meticulous and knowledgeable proof editing.

Contents

1

Key Characters

DCI Greg Geldard and
DS Chris Mathews both from Norfolk police, on a camping holiday

Cornwall Police

Constable Zeal from the Bude police station
Sergeant Sandy Tucker ditto
DI Challinor ditto
Sergeant Nicholl from the Helston police station
Constable Trevelyan ditto

Fellow Campers

Debbie Lowson and her father Mr Lowson
Bruce Harrington owner of Fang and Flossie

Miscellaneous Others

Mr Jones Morwenstow campsite owner
Kim Jones his daughter
Barry Porthleven bar worker
Joe Hawkins Porthleven fisherman

2

Glossary

OIC Officer in Charge

Agley misquoted from the poem 'To a Mouse' by Robert Burns – the best laid schemes of mice and men gang aft agley

Grockles Cornish term for tourists

3

Setting off

Chris was missing in action. She had slipped away while Greg had been subjected to the detailed introduction to their home for the next week, delivered in excruciating detail by the 'campervan hire operative'.

After the final detailed instructions on the chemical loo – emptying of – and the handover of the substantial booklet that apparently explained everything the operative had just covered in his twenty-minute monologue, he went looking. He found her gazing up in admiration at the largest motorhome in the collection.

'I still think we should have gone for one of these,' she said as he walked over. 'Do you think it's too late to change? Look, it's got a king-size bed over the cab, separate dining and lounge areas, TV, separate shower...'

'And it's eight metres long,' said Greg with a shudder. 'And look at the width! It'll never go down the Cornish lanes.' He took her elbow to steer her firmly in the direction of their rather more modest campervan. 'Ours has a TV too,' he said.

'But we'll have to make up the bed every night,' she argued, twisting to look over her shoulder at the sparkling behemoth.

'Zipping two sleeping bags together isn't going to take long,' he replied. 'It's part of the fun of camping. Along with peace and quiet, cooking on a barbecue, sleeping under the stars...'

'The spiders in the campsite shower and emptying the loo,' added Chris.

'Yes, about the latter, I suggest we don't use it except for a middle-of-the-night emergency,' said Greg, with a strong feeling he knew who would be emptying it. 'Hang on, where do you think you're going?'

Chris paused in the act of climbing into the driving seat. 'Getting in the cab, of course.'

'I'm driving,' Greg said firmly. 'I know we put you on the drivers' list but that was in case of emergencies. You just sit back and enjoy the ride.'

Chris regarded him in silence for a moment, then gave way with suspicious alacrity.

'OK,' she said, 'just as you like.' And she walked meekly round the van to the passenger side.

She waved cheerily to the 'operative' as Greg performed an immaculate twelve-point turn to extract the van from its parking slot, then waved again in reassurance as he slightly misjudged the turning circle of the longer-than-he-was-used-to vehicle and missed scraping the passenger side on the gatepost by a generous few millimetres.

When they'd decided on a campervan trip to Cornwall for their first joint holiday from their busy roles in Norfolk Constabulary, they'd discussed almost everything: the type of van, their holiday itinerary, the potential impacts of weather, insects, traffic. The one thing they hadn't discussed was ... who was driving. It now appeared that both had made assumptions.

Roughly five miles down the road from the Norfolk Holiday Vans depot, shortly after they'd missed their turning to the A11 because Greg was distracted by a near miss with the mirrors of a bus coming the other way, Chris pointed in a peremptory fashion at a hardstanding in a field on their left – probably used for sugar beet collection in winter.

'Park there,' she commanded.

Assuming she had some personal emergency on hand, Greg did as he was told and pulled up with a sigh of relief.

Chris turned in her seat and prodded him in the chest with her finger. 'OK,' she said, 'I'm driving. No arguments, please. I love you to bits, but I can't take the stress of seeing the hedge approaching my face every few yards. We haven't made it out of Norfolk yet, and the tension has already given me a pelvic floor you could bounce rocks off.'

Greg surveyed her in silence. He knew that tone and the futility of argument. Privately deciding that a few minutes of discovering it wasn't as easy as she thought would resolve things, he spread his hands in surrender.

'OK,' he said. 'Have it your way.'

The changeover was effected in moments. Chris took a few more to acquaint herself with the layout of the controls, reactivated Google Maps on her phone, and glanced round her.

'OK. Off we go,' she said.

'Please turn around, when possible,' pronounced Google. Chris drove forward to the edge of the concrete pad and, spinning the steering wheel with the flat of her hand in the manner of a long-distance lorry driver, neatly reversed, then in one smooth turn swung the van back onto the road in the opposite direction. Greg watched, open-mouthed.

The remaining few miles to the dual carriageway were accomplished with smooth efficiency and, as Chris neatly inserted their vehicle into the flow of traffic between a slow-moving tractor and a huge articulated truck, Greg found himself relaxing in his seat.

Chris broke the silence. 'I gave up my HGV licence after I stopped driving the farm lorries at harvest,' she remarked conversationally. 'But it all comes back to you pretty quickly.'

'And you didn't think to mention this because...?' he asked.

'Just thought I'd wait and see if you were going to be chauvinist about the driving.'

'Is the copilot permitted to adjust the radio?' Greg enquired.

She flashed him a grin. 'Of course. And the aircon, please..'

'You sure you don't mind doing all the driving?'

'Not at all,' she replied. 'In exchange, you can be OIC, waste disposal.'

***

Their first campsite, near Morwenstow on the North Cornwall coast, was one of the best of its kind, immediately dismissing Chris's childhood memories of spiders, dodgy loos and one cold-water tap serving a score of tents. She backed the van neatly onto its designated hardstanding, and Greg bustled round plugging in electrics, turning gas on and digging out the disposable barbecue while Chris retuned the TV.

'I'll cook supper,' he announced, foraging in the fridge for the fillet steaks and corn-on-the-cob they'd brought with them. He turned round with a couple of cold beers in his hand. 'Only fair after you've done all the driving.'

'Sounds more than fair to me,' said Chris. 'But I'll let you get away with it this once. I'll have a little wander round the site, just to stretch my legs, then we can have our drinks outside in the sun and plan tomorrow's visits.'

One of the things they *had* discussed was the difficulty of manoeuvring a large van around country lanes and finding parking spaces. Greg had proposed they take bikes with them. Chris had agreed, subject to *her* bike, at least, benefitting from an electric motor. In the end, they'd both invested in electric-assisted bikes, currently reposing on brackets at the back of the van.

'I vote for popping back into Devon tomorrow, to visit Clovelly,' said Chris. 'We can go to the visitor centre in the van and walk down from there. Then we could go out on the bikes the day after.'

'Sounds good to me,' agreed Greg, checking the details on his iPad. 'There's a brewery outlet too, so we can stock up with local beer and maybe have lunch at the pub in the village.'

'Then Bodmin Moor the day after, before we head for Port Isaac. Here's to a really peaceful break,' said Chris, and they toasted each other with beer before making short work of steak and sweetcorn with salad and crusty bread.

When the early morning calm was shattered with blue flashing lights, Chris had cause to feel that she'd tempted fate.

'Nothing to do with us,' she said, pulling the sleeping bag over her head like a butterfly attempting to return to the chrysalis. She was about as successful.

Greg was already pulling on his jeans and sweater. 'Can't just ignore it. They might need a hand,' he said.

He wasn't the only camper approaching the squad car parked at an angle near the waste disposal area. A woman was sobbing in the arms of a man, and two uniformed officers were trying to hold back a small crowd of half-dressed and dishevelled holidaymakers.

'Please keep back, sir,' said one to Greg as he approached. 'This is a crime scene, and we need to keep it clear.'

Greg held his ID out at arm's length. 'Understood,' he said. 'I'm DCI Geldard of Norfolk police. I'm here on holiday. I don't want to interfere, but if you need a hand, I'd be glad to help.'

The constable scrutinised the warrant card with dawning relief. 'Thank you, sir,' he said. 'We'd welcome some support until our own superiors get here. There's only me and the sarge. We're a bit thin on the ground in these rural parts.'

'Know the feeling,' replied Greg. Watched curiously by his fellow campers, Greg followed the constable towards the bins and skips. They both stopped a few yards away.

'So, tell me, what's the problem, Constable, and how can I help?' asked Greg.

'Constable Zeal,' said the young officer. 'The lady over there' – he nodded to the woman weeping – 'found a dead baby in the waste bin when she went to put some rubbish in early this morning. Apart from the sarge checking it was genuinely dead and a baby, not a doll or something, we've left it in place for Forensics and the doc. We're just trying to preserve the scene now, but it's not easy keeping the onlookers back.'

Greg spotted Chris approaching. 'You might like to let her through,' he said, nodding in Chris's direction. 'That's Detective Sergeant Mathews, also from Norfolk. She's with me, and I'm sure she'll lend a hand.

'Sounds like you've done everything right, so far,' he reassured Constable Zeal. 'Perhaps you can introduce me to your sergeant, and we can take it from there.'

Chris and the hurriedly introduced Sergeant Sandy Tucker arrived simultaneously. Sergeant Tucker, her fair skin flushed with stress and responsibility, was equally pleased to have some help, especially as she had the irascible owner of the campsite in tow. He was more than a little distressed at this interruption to his summer season.

'Thank you for the offer of help, sir, ma'am,' she said. 'Our team are at least half an hour away and there's no help any closer. I appreciate the support. It's next to impossible to secure the scene effectively with only two of us. I haven't interviewed the lady who found the body, other than a few words, and this gentleman' – she indicated the site owner – 'is worried about his other guests.' She could have added *And his trade!* but didn't need to, given his harassed expression.

'I don't want to be awkward...' said the man who the night before had welcomed Greg and Chris to the site. Greg thought the phrase was up there with *I don't mean to be rude...* as one which was invariably followed by the opposite behaviour. '...but some of my campers are due to leave today and others will be arriving. You can't just close the gates like this.'

'On the basis of what Sergeant Tucker has just described to me,' said Chris to Greg in an undertone, 'I think she was right to ensure that no people or vehicles leave this site. It sounds very much as though the baby is a newborn, and therefore could have been born on site. The mother may still be here.'

'You can't just detain all my guests,' interrupted the owner, whose hearing was apparently exceedingly acute.

'I'm afraid we can,' said Greg briefly. 'What we need you to do now is to lock that gate and wait there for the local officers to arrive. Can you do that for us?'

Oddly, giving him something to do seemed to calm the troubled waters a little, and he went off dutifully, accompanied by Constable Zeal.

Greg turned to Sergeant Tucker. 'You are, of course, in charge until your boss arrives,' he said. 'We have no jurisdiction here. But would you like to tell me what you've done so far, and where we can help?'

'I would, sir, thank you,' she said with a tone of relief. 'And please call me Sandy.

'When we got here, the lady over there was doing pretty much what she's doing now: sobbing in the arms of that man. She didn't say much that was comprehensible, but he told me he'd arrived at the rubbish bins just as she lifted the lid on one, screamed and said she'd seen a dead baby. He looked in the bin, saw she seemed to be right and pulled her away a little before ringing 999. We were in the area so despatch sent us here and we arrived about five or six minutes later. The man is a Mr Bruce Harrington, and the woman is Debbie Lowson. I don't believe they'd met before she took to using him as a handkerchief.' It was apparent that Sandy Tucker wasn't impressed by Debbie Lowson.

'I took a quick look in the bin and saw an apparently dead newborn baby, still with its umbilical cord attached. I touched its neck to check for a pulse, and that it wasn't some bizarre doll, then reported to HQ and told Zeal to keep the crowds back. That's about it.'

'OK,' said Greg, mindful of the need to avoid stepping on local toes. 'I'd say the priorities are to sit Ms Lowson and Mr Harrington down somewhere private to take preliminary statements. Then take a quick look round the shower block and at least rule that out, or in, as the location of the birth. Then we wait for your team. Are you happy with that?'

'Yes, sir. Mr Jones said we could use the site office. It's over there.'

'Yes, we know where it is. How about you and I take a look round the shower block while Sergeant Mathews takes Lowson and Harrington to the office and sits down with them? And do call me Greg,' he added.

'Thank you, sir ... Greg. That sounds fine. I have some gloves and overshoes in my car.'

Chris nodded to Greg, indicated she had her phone with her, and went over to the sobbing lady and increasingly uncomfortable-looking man. 'This way,' she said in a brisk but kindly tone, and, taking Ms Lowson's arm, peeled her off her human box of tissues and led her towards the site office. Mr Harrington followed, an expression of relief on his face.

A quick rummage in the boot of Sandy's car, and both she and Greg were equipped with overshoes and gloves plus, to Greg's approval, paper overalls. Now properly attired, they went to the shower block, past the rubbish bins currently bathed in both the flickering blue light from her squad car and the sunlight now peeping over the tall conifer hedge that split the site in two.

'Do you want to look in the bin?' Sandy asked Greg. 'The lid's up.'

'I'll just take a quick look, but I don't want to compromise your investigation so I won't touch anything,' he promised. The two of them went over to the row of bins. There were five in total, of various colours, depending on what sort of waste they were intended to hold. It was the middle, black, bin that had its lid up. Before approaching, Greg surveyed the ground, but it was relatively new tarmac with no obvious signs of footprints. At the bin, he stopped with his hands firmly by his sides and peered in. As Sandy had described, he saw a small baby curled on its side, its umbilical cord clearly visible. Its eyes were closed and its skin waxy, pale. Without touching the bin, he tried to look closer, the daylight now strongly illuminating the sad sight. The baby was resting on a pile of black plastic sacks, and there appeared to have been no attempt to hide its presence. Nor was it wrapped in anything.

'What are you looking for?' asked Sandy. 'Have I missed anything?'

'I don't think so,' he replied. 'It or, I think, probably she – I couldn't see very well – looks exactly as you described her. I was just wondering whether I could see any sign of post-mortem lividity without moving or touching her. It would tell us whether she's been dead for long. But I can't see anything, so we'll have to leave that to the pathologist.

'Come on, let's have that quick look in the showers.'

He and Sandy walked round the corner and into the ladies' shower block, poking their heads into each toilet and shower cubicle.

'Aha! Over here!' Sandy called.

Greg joined her at a door halfway down the block. The floor of the cubicle was liberally spattered with blood, and there was more on the toilet seat. Leaning in as far as he could, Greg saw what looked like an afterbirth blocking the toilet, as though someone had tried to flush it away. Handfuls of toilet paper had obviously been used in an attempt to clean up, although not very effectively. He stepped back and looked at the floor of the open area that led to the other end of the block and the showers.

'Sandy,' he said. 'Step carefully along here, back to the entrance. I think there may be traces of blood between here and the showers. Your forensic team will need to take a careful look. If I'm right, the mother probably had a shower after giving birth. We need to find her asap. She'll probably need medical care.'

Sandy looked where he was indicating. In the poor, flickering, strip light, it was hard to be sure, but she agreed with his assessment. 'I'll follow you out,' she said. 'We can wait outside for the rest of the team.'

In the campsite office, Chris was sitting down with Ms Lowson. She'd suggested to Mr Harrington that he might like to turn the complimentary coffee machine on and help himself to a cup. Then she nodded over to the far corner of the shop area and advised him to sit there. He'd agreed with an alacrity that suggested he was regretting his compassionate response to the lady in distress. She returned her attention to Ms Lowson, now hiccupping in the aftermath of her tears. She saw a plump woman of around the late thirties clad in a voluminous dressing gown and with plastic sliders on her feet.

Chris set her phone to record and put it down on the coffee table in front of them. 'I'm Sergeant Mathews of Norfolk police,' she said into the mass of dishevelled long hair obscuring the face of the woman in front of her. 'And I'm told you are Ms Debbie Lowson. Is that right?'

The woman nodded, then said, 'Yes,' in a whisper which Chris hoped the recording had captured.

'I understand you've had a distressing experience. Can you tell me about it?'

The woman drew a shuddering sigh and looked up for a moment. 'It was awful,' she said. 'Just awful.'

'I'm sure it was,' said Chris. 'What time did you go to the bins?'

'I don't know! How should I know that?'

'I just thought you might have noticed the time,' said Chris soothingly. 'It must have been very early.'

'I suppose it was,' said Ms Lowson, calming down a little. 'I woke early, so I thought I'd take the rubbish from under our motorhome to the bins, and pop into the loos while I was at it. If you leave garbage lying around, the seagulls get it you know. And they make a terrible mess.'

'So, did you go into the toilet block first?' asked Chris.

'No, I went to the bins first. And when I lifted the lid I saw, I saw...' She gulped and started crying again.

Chris didn't know whether it was prejudice engendered by the semi-hysterical tears or instinct, but she couldn't help feeling that some of the distress was histrionics.

'You must be pretty desperate for the loo by now then,' she said, her practical streak coming to the fore.

'You know, I'd forgotten about it,' said the woman. 'I'm OK for the moment. But if you've finished, perhaps I could go back to the toilet block.'

'I'm afraid you probably won't be able to use those,' said Chris. 'They may be a crime scene. Perhaps there are some others around here that you can use. I'll ask the owner in a minute.

'First, can you manage a few more questions? Are you here on your own?'

'No, I'm here with my dad. He'll be getting worried,' she said, as though she'd only just remembered him. 'I need to go and talk to him.'

'You'll need to talk to the Cornwall police first,' said Chris. 'I'm sure they'll be here in a moment, and then I'll make sure your father is told where you are. Ah, here's the owner back again. Mr Jones, are there any toilets in here?' she asked him. 'Ms Lowson here needs one and, of course, she can't use the main block.'

'Through here,' he replied, lifting part of the counter and waving her through to the back of the shop. 'Just through there, on the right.

'More police have just arrived,' he said with a grimace, as though he wasn't very pleased about it. They'll be here in a moment.'

They were, in fact, talking to Greg outside. Inspector Challinor was a hard-faced woman with a brisk manner. Although polite, she didn't seem best pleased to find Greg and Chris on her patch, and Greg was left with a strong feeling that had he not outranked her, he would have received short shrift.

'Thank you for your help, sir,' she was saying. 'But we'll deal with this now. You must be keen to get back to your holiday, you and Sergeant Mathews. I don't think this will take too long to clear up.'

She walked into the campsite office, leaving the door open behind her so Greg had a clear view of what happened next.

'Thank you, Sergeant Mathews. I've just told your ... I've just told Chief Inspector Geldard that we can take matters from here. Jones,' she said, addressing the site owner. 'Where's your daughter?'

'My daughter?' The choler rose again, flushing his face, and he visibly bristled. 'What the hell do you mean, where's my daughter? What's this got to do with her?'

'Just what we'd like to know,' said Inspector Challinor. 'She's usually at the bottom of anything going off round here, you must admit. Where is she?'

4

Next steps

With quite extraordinary expedition, Chris and Greg found themselves thanked and, metaphorically speaking, out the door.

Greg managed a brief handover, explaining what he and Sergeant Tucker had found in the shower block but gave up on outlining his theory, as it clearly wasn't wanted.

Chris was displaced from the site office with even scanter courtesy, but found the time to collect an email address from Constable Zeal to which she could send the recording of her interview with Debbie Lowson. She had little confidence it would be listened to, and the two of them retired to a safe distance, a few yards from their campervan. From there, they watched as one of the newly arrived constables was despatched to the owner's farmhouse on the top of the hill to fetch his daughter.

A silence fell on the area as Greg and Chris exchanged glances then, with silent agreement, returned to their van.

Chris put the kettle on, and Greg burrowed into the fridge for milk and butter.

'Toast?' he asked. 'It feels like it's well past breakfast even though it's still only...' He looked at his watch. 'Christ, it's only seven-thirty.'

They settled down with coffee and hot, buttered toast, conversation dilatory, and with one eye on the scene developing by the site offices. They saw the constable return with a half-dressed and wholly disgruntled teenager in tow.

'They might have given her chance to get dressed properly,' remarked Chris, noting the dark hoodie, obviously hurriedly pulled on over slightly-too-small pyjamas. Her hair was towsled and her bare feet were pushed into battered slippers, one of which came off as she was pushed down the slope towards the offices.

'I don't understand why they seem so sure she's involved,' said Greg, putting more bread in the toaster. 'OK, I realise I don't know the backstory, but nothing about that girl fits with what I saw in the shower block.'

'Which was what?' asked Chris. 'You haven't told me yet.'

'First, the birth clearly took place in one of the toilet cubicles. There's blood all over the place and what looks like afterbirth in the pan.

'Second, there's a blood trail down the block from the toilet cubicles to the shower, and I'm pretty sure the forensic experts will find evidence the mother took a shower before leaving the block.

'Now, why would the girl who lives on site, and presumably has a perfectly functioning bathroom in her own home, take the risk of using the campers' shower block?'

'To avoid her father noticing what was going on?' suggested Chris.

'Perhaps,' conceded Greg. 'But, if so, how did she get from the shower block to her home without any of us noticing? Judging by the blood I saw, the birth had taken place pretty recently, not hours ago.

'Moreover, did the girl we've just watched struggling with a police constable look like she'd been through a devastating physical event like giving birth on her own? She was showing no signs of physical discomfort, no signs of bleeding, and she just looked really cross rather than distressed. OK, she's fairly big in the belly, but so are a lot of teenagers, and it's a bit of a leap to assume she's recently given birth from that alone.'

'So, you're thinking the baby was born only a short while before being found in the bin?'

'I am, yes. It'll be very interesting to know what the pathologist says, but it didn't look as though it had been there very long to me. Obviously, I didn't move the body. I didn't even touch her. But I peered as closely as I could, and I couldn't see any lividity in the lower areas.'

'Meaning, she hadn't been in that position for long.'

'Exactly,' said Greg.

A silence fell for a moment, broken only by the crunch of toast and the click as a mug was put down on the table.

Then the peace was shattered by angry shouts and orders to 'Calm down and stop struggling'. They both stood up to get a better view, just in time to see the teenage daughter of the campsite owner spread-eagled across the bonnet of a police car, before being handcuffed then hustled into the back seat. Chris was quite impressed by the language the teenager was using.

'Varied and creative,' she commented. 'There were even a couple of descriptions I might find a use for.'

Greg sat down again, his face thoughtful. 'Looks like they've arrested her,' he said. 'Chris, what did you think of your lachrymose witness? The woman who found the body?'

'Ms Lowson,' said Chris. 'A bit overdramatic for my taste. And poor Mr Harrington, the man she was using as a Kleenex, he was really regretting his kind impulse. I think she was genuinely upset but made too much of it for it to feel wholly genuine.'

'Big girl, was she?' asked Greg. 'I couldn't see her very well under the dressing gown.'

'Plump,' said Chris, then looked at Greg sharply. 'You're seeing her as the mother?' she asked.

'Possible, isn't it?' said Greg. 'If we're investigating a murder, who do we look at very closely?'

'The family,' said Chris. 'And the person who finds the body.' She spaced out the last four words, thoughtfully. 'You think that when Mr Harrington came upon her, she'd just put the baby in the bin, rather than opened it to put rubbish in?'

'Possible, isn't it?' said Greg again. 'For that matter, where's the rubbish she says she brought to the waste area?'

'She said she was there so early in the morning because she woke up, needed to pay a visit to the loo, and thought she might as well move the rubbish at the same time because the seagulls make such a mess of it,' said Chris.

'So where is it? She didn't put it in on top of the baby. Has anyone checked any of the other bins? Did anyone see her dispose of rubbish?'

'No idea. I doubt it. Inspector Challinor seemed to arrive with her mind made up, and her theory doesn't involve any campers.'

'Did you have a chat with Harrington?' asked Greg.

'No. I didn't have the chance,' said Chris.

'Then, I think a little chat with Mr Harrington might be in order, along with a look round for Ms Lowson's missing rubbish.'

With the departure of Inspector Challinor, her arrestee, the mortuary van carrying the baby, and most of the forensic team, the pitch of excitement started to diminish from frantic through electrified and down to a more reasonable level of energised as Chris and Greg set off round the site on the hunt for Mr Harrington. There was a lot more chit-chat than would normally be the case amongst naturally reserved British campers, and a lot of exchanging of teas and coffees for hot gossip. Mr Harrington was easy to spot holding court outside his vintage yellow and pink VW campervan, his bald head shining slightly in the dawn glow.

'Well, it would have to be outside, wouldn't it,' responded Chris to Greg when he pointed this out. 'Given that the van already contains a Great Dane and what looks remarkably like a dire wolf, there's not a lot of room for anyone else inside.'

Mr Harrington seemed to be enjoying his five minutes of local fame and, if anything, appeared to consider that further association with Chris and Greg could only enhance his standing with fellow campers. He made his excuses to his current audience and encouraged them to take their coffees elsewhere, to allow him to sit down with Chris and Greg in relative privacy at the table by his van.

'Call me Bruce,' he said sociably. The two huge canine heads, one smooth, the other thickly furred, continued to observe them through the side windows.

'If you want to let the dogs out, we don't mind,' said Greg, thinking that they looked as though they could do with some fresh air.

'I think I might, now the crowds have dispersed,' said Bruce. 'Fang gets a bit nervous in a crowd.'

Chris looked less than enthusiastic about a close encounter with a nervous wolf apparently named Fang, but both dogs turned out to be lovable, and biddable, giants. Moreover, the Great Dane was Fang; the dire wolf was introduced as Flossie. Greg decided that Bruce either had a quirky sense of humour or none at all. He couldn't quite make his mind up which.

'You met me earlier,' said Chris. 'This is my partner, Detective Chief Inspector Greg Geldard.'

'Pleased to meet you,' said Bruce. 'Are you from Norfolk too?'

'That's right,' said Greg, rubbing the furry tummy that Flossie had offered him. 'We're just on holiday, as I'm sure Chris explained. But I had a couple of questions, if you didn't mind. Entirely unofficial,' he added hurriedly. 'But as I'm sure you can imagine, it's hard to switch off entirely, especially when a crime happens right under your nose.'

'I don't mind,' said Bruce, reaching into his van and returning with a large cafetière full of coffee. 'Want a drink while we talk? I just made this.'

'Thank you,' said Greg. 'Black for us both, please. You were up very early this morning. Was there a particular reason?'

'I'm always an early riser,' said Bruce, pouring coffee and offering sugar. 'I normally take the dogs for a walk before I go to work, so it's habit.'

'What do you do?' asked Chris, sipping her coffee and noting with regret that it could have been hotter.

'I'm a solicitor in Cambridge,' said Bruce. 'Nothing special. Wills and probate mainly.'

'I'm particularly interested in what you saw of Ms Lowson before she opened the waste bin—' said Greg.

'I didn't see her open it,' interrupted Bruce. 'The first thing I saw was her rushing towards me, and after that I couldn't see anything much because she was crying all over me. My shirt's still wet,' he added, plucking at the shoulder of his polo shirt with a look of distaste.

'Can we get this clear?' said Greg. 'You walked from here over to the waste area...'

'I was heading for the loos,' said Bruce. 'But from this part of the site, you pass the waste bins first. I was just coming up the slope there,' – he pointed to where police tape now fluttered – 'when this woman started screaming, then ran towards me and flung herself at me. She's no lightweight either,' he added feelingly. 'Nearly bowled me over. Good job I didn't have Fang with me. He'd have had her.'

Chris, currently being licked into submission by Fang, looked a little sceptical but held her tongue.

'Which way was she facing when you first saw her?' asked Greg.

'Away from me, I think. Towards the bin. I think she was looking into it. Then she turned, saw me, and galloped down the slope to me, like I said.'

'Did you see whether she had any bags of rubbish with her?'

'No,' said Bruce after a pause. 'No, I don't think so. They're very good at keeping things tidy here. It's a very well-run site. I think I'd have noticed if there'd been rubbish on the ground.'

'Did you look in the bin?'

'Not me,' said Bruce emphatically. 'Not after what she told me she'd seen. I didn't go any closer at all. It wouldn't have been easy even if I'd wanted to,' he added, 'given I was being cried all over by what felt like an all-in wrestler.'

'What d'you mean?' asked Chris. 'Was she pushing you away?'

'Was she pushing me?' exclaimed Bruce. 'If she'd leaned on me any more, we'd both have been flat on our backs in the yard. I was so relieved when you arrived and took control,' he said. 'I was definitely out of my depth. Weeping women aren't my thing. Especially,' he hesitated.

'Especially?' prompted Chris.

'It's a bit unkind in the circs,' said Bruce, a little shamefaced. 'But I was going to say, especially one who smelled a bit odd.'

'In what way?' asked Chris. 'BO?'

'No, not really. Sort of metallic. Just odd.'

It took Greg and Chris a little while to extricate themselves from Bruce's impromptu coffee morning, but when they did eventually get away, they headed, without discussion, up the campsite, away from their van and towards the farmhouse at the top of the field.

'You thinking what I'm thinking?' asked Greg.

'Ms Debbie Lowson,' said Chris. 'You're thinking that she didn't find the baby, she put it there, then realised she'd been seen by Bruce Harrington.'

'And the odd smell?'

'Could have been blood,' said Chris. 'If she'd only just given birth, she might well still have been bleeding.'

'So why didn't anyone notice when she was in the office? Did you smell anything?'

'No, but I didn't get as close to her as poor Bruce,' replied Chris. 'And Inspector Challinor was only interested in Jones's daughter. But Lowson did go to the toilet shortly after we got into the office. In fact, I made that easy for her.' She explained the circumstances.

'It would be interesting to take a look in the office toilets,' said Greg. 'And even more interesting to have another chat with Ms Lowson.'

'If she'd talk to us,' said Chris. 'We have no authority here remember, and she's got no reason to want to talk to us, particularly if she's hiding something.'

'And Inspector Challinor won't abandon her theory easily,' said Greg. 'Not now she's nailed her colours to the mast.'

'Surely a doctor's examination will rule out Miss Jones easily enough?'

'I'd have thought so,' agreed Greg. 'Problem is, where will Ms Lowson be by then. If she absconds, she may not be easy to find.'

'Isn't she here with her father? Perhaps we could have a chat with him.'

By this time, they had reached the hedge that divided the campsite from the farmhouse garden and were pounced upon by the owner.

'Did you see what they did?' he demanded. 'Did you see what they did to my daughter? It's a disgrace. She's done nothing. Nothing. I shall make a formal complaint, and I hope you'll back me up.' He paused for breath, and Greg seized the opportunity.

'You know we have no jurisdiction here,' he said. 'But I must admit, I didn't understand what Inspector Challinor has against your daughter.'

'Nothing but teenage mischief,' interjected the distraught father. 'She seemed to have taken some ecstasy at a pop concert a couple of years ago, although there was some doubt over whether she actually had and, if she had, whether she was slipped it in a drink. Unfortunately, she didn't learn from that mistake and got caught growing pot in our greenhouse about six months ago. That landed her with a police caution. I couldn't have been more mad,' he added. 'It was so stupid. Part of some idiotic bet, I think, and there was literally *one* plant. But it brought her to the attention of the police again, and Inspector Challinor took it upon herself to give her a lecture as well as a caution. That did not go well.'

Recalling the language used when the youngster was arrested, Chris could imagine. 'What's your daughter's name?' she asked.

'Kim. Well, she was christened Kate Jones, but that wasn't groovy enough apparently. I blame the crowd she's in for everything,' he said. 'But even so, she's not a bad lass. Just a bit impetuous. And more to the point, not pregnant! I'd have noticed. I mean, God, I may be a man, but I'm not blind. And I've had a wife and sisters. I know when a woman is having her period, and Kim had one just a couple of weeks ago.'

'She could have been faking it,' said Chris. 'Just to play devil's advocate,' she added hurriedly.

'I suppose she could have,' said her father. 'But if so, she did a very thorough job. Not just rolling around complaining of pains, but all the moodiness as well.'

'Anyway,' said Greg. 'If she hasn't given birth, and I have to say I'm with you on this, a medical examination will make that clear immediately, and she should be home with you very soon.'

'I should think so too. And I'll be complaining, as I said earlier. Anyway, I must get myself over to the police station and find out what's happening to Kim. She threw a tantrum at the mere suggestion I come with her, but I can't hang around here any longer.

'Now, why were you headed up here? Did you want to see me? Was it urgent?'

'Not exactly. We were hoping to have a chat with Ms Lowson or her father. Chris here was a bit worried about her, as she seemed to be so upset,' Greg added, slightly mendaciously.

'They're over there,' said Mr Trent. 'They wanted to leave. Packed up and everything, but the police said no one is to leave the site just yet so I'm stuck with a lot of unhappy campers, and there'll be a second lot soon, what with all today's potential arrivals stuck in the entrance. I hope the police get their act together soon, or they'll bankrupt me.'

Greg and Chris exchanged glances. 'So we're stuck here too,' said Greg, unsurprised. 'In that case, we might as well see if we can have a chat with Ms Lowson.'

Greg and Chris headed over to the large campervan indicated by the site owner. It was near the exit, the awning tucked away and the space around it completely clear of the usual deckchairs and camping table.

'They certainly look as though they're ready to depart,' said Chris as she reached up to knock on the side door. It opened before she had a chance.

'Yes?' snapped the man in the doorway. 'Unless you're here to tell us we can leave, we're not interested.'

'Hi, I'm Chris Mathews,' said Chris. 'I was talking to your daughter last night, and I just wanted to check she was OK. She was understandably very upset.' She could see a shadow of a shape behind the irascible man in front of her. He was, she judged, around sixty-ish, stout and short. Dressed in tightly stretched jeans and jumper, he bore a distinct similarity to a well-stuffed sausage.

'I see,' he said unpleasantly. 'You're the police from Norfolk, sticking your noses in. As I understand it, you have no rights here.'

'Other than as a woman, concerned for another woman, no I don't,' said Chris. The shadow behind Mr Lowson moved forward a little, until she was in the brighter light from the open door. She caught Chris's eye, nodded her head sideways twice, then stepped back.

'I'm sorry we disturbed you,' said Greg, who had also witnessed the silent byplay. 'We'll leave you in peace.' He tapped Chris on the shoulder and, joining in with the silent nodding, jerked his head towards the site offices and indicated they should move away. The door slammed as they turned their backs.

'Chris,' said Greg, 'I think she wants to talk to you.'

'I thought so too,' she replied. 'I'm going to head over to the loo in the office. She might join me there. If she does and that horrible father tries to follow, can you run interference?'

'My pleasure,' said Greg with a grin.

When Chris pushed the door to the site office open, it appeared to be deserted. She went in quietly, looking to left and right, then headed for the ladies' toilets. As she waited by the handbasins, noticing as she did so that her hair gave a general impression of having been dragged through a hedge backwards, she made a half-hearted attempt to sort out the tangle with her fingers, then saw in the mirror the dumpy figure of Ms Lowson entering the block.

'Hi,' said Chris, turning towards her. 'Are you OK? That must have been a very distressing experience for you. This morning, I mean.' She deliberately left vague precisely what the experience might have been. 'Can I call you Debbie?' she added. 'I'm Chris. I work for Norfolk police, as I said earlier. But I'm on holiday here, like you.'

Debbie didn't meet her eyes but came to the handbasins to rinse her hands under the hot tap. 'Not exactly like me,' she said with a world of bitterness in her tone. 'You're with that rather gorgeous detective and I'm with my father. And yes, it was upsetting.' She turned and leaned back on the basin, but still looking down at the floor.

'I thought you might like to talk,' said Chris. 'You'd be very welcome to come back to our van for a coffee and a chat. Sometimes it helps to talk.'

'I'd...' Debbie paused. 'I thought... Could I?' she managed finally. 'I'd like to explain, but I don't think my father will let me.'

'Why should he stop you?' asked Chris. 'It's just coffee, not cocaine! Come on.' She took Debbie by the elbow and towed her, unresisting, from the office and across to their hired campervan. Out of the corner of her eye she saw Greg hovering near the Lowsons' rather smarter motorhome. Just as she ushered Debbie into their tiny holiday space and urged her to take a seat, she saw Mr Lowson pop out as though fired from a gun. He started to head across the site towards them but was intercepted by Greg.

Standing over the kettle, waiting for it to boil, Chris watched as Greg engaged the red-faced man in conversation. It didn't seem as though Mr Lowson was inclined to talk. Although the words were inaudible to Chris, it was apparent he was impatient at the interference, and when Greg went so far as to take his elbow and attempt to turn him towards the site office, he was shaken off brusquely. Lowson's voice rose until it was audible, the words obscure but the temper clear.

'I said he wouldn't like me talking to you,' said Debbie from her seat in the corner. 'He doesn't like me talking to anyone.'

There came a sharp rap on the side door. 'Debbie, I know you're in there. Come out at once.'

Chris hesitated. What she wanted to say was *You don't have to do what he says, you can stay and talk to me if you want to*. But the fact that she knew very little about the

Lowsons and their family set-up impeded her tongue. Then the opportunity was gone. Debbie got up and sidled past Chris to the door.

'Here, take my card,' muttered Chris in an undertone. 'You can always ring me if you like.'

Debbie took it, with a quick glance at Chris, and tucked into a pocket as she reached the door and opened it. 'Coming father,' she said in a tone designed for appeasement.

'And, you pair,' said the angry voice outside. 'You can take your long noses and stick them in someone else's business. They're not wanted here.'

Just as Chris followed Debbie to the door, she saw him seize her arm and hustle her away across the site. Greg was standing alongside, and half made a move to intervene, then thought better of it. His arm dropped to his side, and he came up the steps just as the kettle started it's *I am boiling* song.

'Sorry, Chris. I did try to intercept, but short of performing a citizen's arrest, it wasn't going to work. Problem is,' he said as he picked up the kettle and poured the boiling water into two mugs, 'he's not in any way hampered by normal standards of politeness. He clearly thinks nothing of riding roughshod over anyone, family or stranger. He was downright rude to me.'

'And he's bullying his daughter,' said Chris. 'I wonder what else is going on there?'

***

It was early afternoon when the message came round that movement controls were lifted and campers who wished to move on were free to do so provided they left contact details with the police officer on the gate.

'Seems a bit premature,' commented Greg. 'Not sure I'd have wanted to lose all my witnesses so quickly. Still, perhaps they know something we don't.'

The Lowson motorhome was first out of the gate. Not surprisingly, as it had been waiting, silent and ready, for the past couple of hours. Debbie Lowson had not reappeared and was only faintly visible behind the tinted screen as they pulled out, her father driving.

Greg and Chris packed up their van and were also heading for the exit when a police car pulled in from the main road and decanted a defiant young lady – still mouthing off. Chris leaped out of the driving seat as though propelled by an ejector.

'Kim, hi!' she said, joining the angry young woman on the forecourt as the police car hurried away. 'I just wanted to check you're OK.'

'And who the ff— are you?' asked Kim, making a late decision to moderate her language.

'Chris. I'm on holiday here, but I'm also with Norfolk police, AND I THINK YOU'VE HAD A ROUGH DEAL,' she said loudly over the mouthing-off that was provoked by the word 'police'.

Kim paused a moment, and Chris added into the temporary lull, 'Your dad explained the situation. If you'd like to chat, get any advice, we're here.'

As Kim hesitated, her father came rushing out of the site reception office.

'Kim,' he said, wrapping her in a big hug. 'Thank God. Leaving you there is the hardest thing you've ever asked me to do.'

'Nothing you could do,' said Kim, shrugging, but Chris felt that the bravado was mostly put on and the teenager was only moments from tears.

'Come on in,' urged Bill Jones. 'Come on in, all of you. These are the proverbial good cops,' he said to his daughter. 'Maybe they can help.'

At a nod from Chris, Greg climbed down from their van and followed the trio into reception. Lifting part of the front desk, Bill waved them through into the back room. 'Hot chocolate?' he said to Kim. 'Coffee?' he offered to Greg and Chris, much to Greg's relief – he was strongly of the opinion that the only respectable form for chocolate was a big solid block in a purple wrapper, and that as a drink it was the spawn of the devil.

They all made themselves comfortable in the shabby back room, pushing papers aside to make space on a three-legged sofa propped up at one corner with a brick, a desk chair with the stuffing escaping and a lone dining chair. Greg was unlucky enough to get the dining chair, and very hard it was. Chris swivelled on the creaky desk chair, while father and daughter huddled up on the sofa. Bill passed a packet of custard creams around, tried to put his arm round Kim, was firmly repulsed and sat back looking at Greg with a silent appeal.

'Kim, I'm Greg. I work in Norfolk police too, which puts me in a slightly delicate position, as I'm just on holiday here. But I have to say that I was very, very surprised when you were arrested. I struggled to see how it was justified, and I'm still struggling. I assume the medical examination cleared you.'

Kim flushed. 'Yes it did,' she said firmly. 'And as to why I was arrested, that's because that Challinor woman hates me. She's hated me ever since her precious boy got caught with pot, and she blamed me, even though I had nothing to do with it. I only had the one plant, just to win a bet,' she said in a tone of immense grievance. 'He had packets of the stuff. But it was me that got the caution.'

'So it was personal?' asked Chris.

'Sure was,' said Kim. 'And most of them there know it. But they still did that horrible creepy examination and took samples and everything.'

'Samples?' asked Chris.

'DNA, they said. And blood samples, to see if I was under the influence. Which I wasn't! I've got a match on Saturday!'

'Kim plays with the Devon under-eighteens team,' said Bill proudly. 'Football.'

By the time Greg and Chris made their farewells, Kim had simmered down a bit and Bill Jones was ringing the local police and crime commissioner with his complaint.

Back in their van and driving them out onto the coast road, Chris glanced sideways at Greg.

'Sorry if that was a bit tricky,' she said. 'But I was worried about the girl. Especially with no mum around to look out for her.'

'Yes. Where is her mum?' asked Greg. 'I didn't like to ask, in the circumstances.'

'Dead some years ago, apparently. It's been just her and her dad for some time, and I think she looks out for him as much as he does for her. At least, that's what she said when we popped off to the ladies together.'

'I wondered what was taking so long,' remarked Greg. 'Half this case seems to be taking place in the ladies' loo! Did she say anything else of interest?'

'Not really. Just that she'd overheard one of the constables say the DNA analysis was being rushed through, but that was all.'

'Can we now get back to our holiday? After all these delays, I suggest we abandon Clovelly this time and head straight for Port Isaac,' said Greg. 'And hopefully, no more alarms in the night.'

'I'm still worried about Debbie Lowson,' said Chris. 'But I suppose there's not much we can do about that.'

5

Next stop

The drive to the campsite near Port Isaac was accomplished without incident, and although the site was less sophisticated than the first, it benefitted from lots of space and extensive views across the river valley towards Wadebridge.

While Greg completed his self-imposed duties relating to setting up camp, Chris went to check out the on-site cafe serving cream teas. She was soon chatting with the friendly lady who had just pulled the latest batch of floury scones from the oven.

'The bad news is,' she announced to Greg on her return to their campervan, 'cream teas are over for today, and the local advice is, don't, under any circumstances, take a van into Port Isaac unless we want to spend the rest of the summer wedged there.'

'Makes sense to me,' said Greg, looking up from his iPad. 'I've just been googling Port Isaac, and I'm not sure I'd want to take a quad bike there, let alone a van. What do they suggest as an alternative?'

'Taxi,' said Chris. 'There are organised trips, but I doubt we'd want to go on one of those. A local taxi can drop us off at the top of the village, and pick us up later, after we've had time to see the sights and have a pub lunch.'

'Sounds good to me,' replied Greg. 'I had been hoping to hear the Fisherman's Friends. You know, the shanty group the film was about, but it seems they don't perform regularly any more. Only occasionally at the pub.'

'Well, we might be lucky,' said Chris. 'Shall we book a taxi then? I've got the phone number of the local firm.'

'Absolutely. And while you do that, I'll get tonight's supper on.'

***

The following day was one of those idyllic times, when everything went right. The sun shone and a gentle, ozone-scented breeze wafted in from the sea as they made their way down the steep streets from the building that had been the village school in the TV series, to the harbour, then up the opposite side of the ravine to the other locations they remembered from the various programmes that had used the picturesque village as a backdrop. Lots of pottering in and out of craft shops followed, more walking up and down steep streets that were narrow enough for outstretched arms to touch both sides, then they retired to the pub and sat in the bar that had figured on both TV and film. With a pint of something Cornish in front of each of them, and looking forward to fish and chips (Greg) and mussels in cider cream (Chris), they simultaneously leaned back, relaxed and sighed.

'Just what the doctor ordered,' said Greg, looking round the bar.

'Won't be sorry when they bring the food though,' said Chris. 'I'm starving. If it doesn't arrive soon, I'll have eaten all the bread and we'll have to order some more.' She took another big bite of the crusty wedge of buttered bread, and washed it down with a gulp of the local lager.

'You won't have any room for the mussels at that rate,' remarked Greg.

'Oh I will, believe me,' said Chris with heartfelt certainty, watching as a plate piled high with golden chips and what appeared to be a battered whale approached their table, accompanied by a big bowl with fragrant steam rising from the top.

Silence fell as they both tucked in with enthusiasm. Over by the bar, a couple of locals were chatting with the landlord while a small group of tourists edged past to sit at tables on the balcony. They were accompanied by a large greyhound, which looked longingly at Greg's chips as it was towed past. Greg watched it with suspicion until it was safely out of range. Chris, on the other hand, was eavesdropping on the group at the bar.

She looked round to see if there was a TV anywhere in sight, but this bar had adopted the civilised approach: it was a TV-free zone.

'Greg,' she said. 'Did you hear what they said just now?'

'Who? No. I was watching that dog. I was sure it was going to make a grab for my chips,' replied Greg, spearing up the last two on his fork as he spoke.

'I think they were talking about the dead baby case,' said Chris. 'Can you check it out on your phone while I finish my mussels. There might be something on BBC iPlayer.'

'No signal,' said Greg, looking at his phone.

'Try the Wi-Fi,' suggested Chris round a mouthful of shellfish and cream sauce. She pointed at the sign behind the bar which gave the password. Greg logged on, scrolled for a moment, then held his phone out so Chris could see as well. The headline was 'Hunt for Missing Mother'. After reading what little fact was present in a lot of words, Greg and Chris looked at each other.

'I said they were letting everyone go prematurely,' said Greg.

'All that really tells us is that Kim is in the clear and they're still looking for the mother,' said Chris. 'But I'd give odds on Debbie Lowson being involved. I wish I'd had a chance to talk to her properly.'

'If they'd hung on just a little longer, they could have compared DNA samples,' said Greg. 'God, it's annoying to see people cock things up. Good job she doesn't work under me. She wouldn't last a day.'

Chris didn't need him to explain he meant Inspector Challinor.

That evening, with mutual agreement that the enormous lunch they'd eaten meant they didn't need supper, they settled down to watch a DVD with glasses of wine to hand and bowls of olives and nuts within easy reach. The peace didn't last long. They'd barely begun to enjoy the brass band music integral to the film – a favourite of Greg's since his time in Yorkshire – when the shrill sound of a mobile phone interrupted proceedings. Reluctantly pausing Ewan McGregor in mid-reminiscence with the character played by Tara Fitzgerald, Greg hunted for his phone and found it under the sleeping bags ready for nightfall.

'Geldard,' he said, then fell silent. He put the phone on speaker, and they both listened as the voice of Sergeant Sandy Tucker explained why she was ringing.

'So, since I was told you'd spoken to her just before they left, I thought she might have given some indication of where they were going.'

'I'm afraid not,' said Chris, swallowing a mouthful of nuts. 'Her father whisked her away just as we were about to have a chat, so sorry, no idea.'

'Ah, her father,' said Sandy. 'What was your impression of him?'

'Rude and aggressive,' said Greg. 'But why are you asking?'

'General impressions can be helpful, don't you find, sir?' she said. 'And you have special experience...' She tailed off.

'Does Inspector Challinor know you're contacting us?' asked Greg bluntly.

'Er, no,' admitted Sandy. 'She left it to me to make contact with departed campers, using the contact details they left with us. She didn't specify how I should go about it. I tried the Lowsons first, but they're not picking up. Then I thought, both because you had helped out that evening and because you'd spoken to the Lowsons...' She tailed off again.

'You have a particular reason for asking about the Lowsons?' asked Greg. 'What is it?'

'Well, it occurred to me, once Kim Jones was out of the picture, that it was possible Debbie Lowson could have put the baby *in* the bin, rather than just discovered it there. And then...' She hesitated again.

'And then?' prompted Greg.

'If I tell you this, sir, it needs to be confidential,' said Sandy. 'Otherwise, I lose my job and probably my pension too. The DNA results are through.'

'But you've nothing to compare them with. Or have you?' asked Greg. In the background, Chris was almost holding her breath.

'No, nothing to compare them with other than the placenta which we recovered from the washroom,' Sandy replied. 'And that did show up something...' She hesitated. '...interesting.' She took a deep breath that was audible down the phone, then said in a rush, 'I didn't know this, but a placenta contains DNA from both parents. And apparently it showed that the father of the baby was also its grandfather.'

There was total silence for a moment while Greg and Chris worked it out.

'You mean, it was the product of incest?' said Greg, getting there first. 'The father of the baby was also the father of its mother?'

'Yes,' said Sandy.

'And hence the interest in the Lowsons and Mr Lowson in particular.'

'Yes,' she said.

6

Moving on

Sandy was quick to qualify her monosyllabic response.

'My interest, anyway.'

'Inspector Challinor doesn't share your view?' asked Chris.

'She says we shouldn't jump to conclusions. That if we narrow the focus of our investigation too quickly, we risk missing something.'

Greg almost blurted something out but stopped himself just in time.

'I'm sorry we can't help, Sandy,' he said. 'But do feel free to ring again, if you like, and we'll certainly get in touch if anything occurs to us. Have you tried seeing if their phone is pinging off any masts?' he added just before they rang off.

'Yes, and nothing. It seems the phone is off.'

His phone silent and the DVD stopped, Greg and Chris looked at one another other. 'Pity Challinor didn't avoid jumping to conclusions where Kim was concerned,' grumbled Chris. 'If she'd conducted a proper investigation in the first place, she'd either have Debbie Lowson safe and her father in custody, or at least she'd have ruled them out. As it is…' Words failed her.

'I agree. I've rarely seen anyone make such a mess of an investigation,' said Greg. 'But just because we didn't like Lowson doesn't mean he's necessarily the abuser. Or that Debbie was the mother just because she was there on the spot and she looked the part. Assuming they are, is just making the same mistake as Challinor.'

'But at least, if she'd done her job properly from the start! Oh, never mind. We've said it all,' said Chris. 'Let's try and put it out of our heads. A right busman's holiday this is threatening to be.'

They did their best. A trip to a model railway left them giggling helplessly when they discovered it was essentially a children's playground, complete with soft play areas and a miniature boating lake. They solemnly rode the train – the only passengers not accompanied by toddlers – and, with some considerable difficulty, extricated their campervan from the surrounding narrow lanes and back onto the main road. They went swimming in a distinctly chilly sea at Perranporth, sunbathed briefly (and optimistically) in the dunes, then warmed themselves up with another gargantuan fish lunch in one of the beachside bars.

'I'll grow fins if I eat much more fish,' observed Chris as their empty plates were cleared away.

'Your fish hasn't had fins,' objected Greg. 'You've had shellfish and crab non-stop ever since we got to Cornwall.'

'That way, you don't get any bones,' explained Chris. 'Plus, it tends to come with more interesting accompaniments than batter plus tartare.'

Greg grinned at her, and toasted her with the dregs of his cider. 'Are you enjoying yourself?' he asked, 'apart from the major crime hiccup at the start of this holiday.'

'Of course I am,' she said, responding to the gesture with the dregs of her low-alcohol lager. 'The only question is, where next? We can do one more stay somewhere down here before we have to turn towards home.'

'How about St Ives?' asked Greg, consulting the map of Cornwall on his phone. 'Arty capital of Cornwall? I think Penzance might be a bit far, but we could do it if you let me drive some of the way.'

'St Ives sounds good to me,' replied Chris. 'And no, that's not because I'm afraid of your driving, although I am, of course.'

'I drove us here OK!' Greg made out he was offended.

'True, but that was mostly on dual carriageways.' Chris tapped his knee. 'You're coming along quite nicely really, considering,' she said with a kindly condescension.

'One more jibe like that, and you empty the loo,' threatened Greg.

They were on the A30, just passing the turning to Truro, when Greg's phone buzzed. As he was taking a turn driving, it was left to Chris to answer it.

'I said you should pair it with the van,' she grumbled as she followed his instructions for the passcode. 'I can never remember this number, as you well know. Why you can't pick something obvious, like my birthday or yours, I don't know. Hello,' she said just before the call went to answerphone. 'This is Chris Mathews answering on behalf of Greg Geldard. He's driving at present and can't...' She stopped and listened for a moment. 'OK, Sandy,' she said. 'I'll put you on speaker. Can you say that again?'

'Lowson, the father I mean, has been found dead in his motorhome. Suspected heart attack.'

'What about Debbie?' interrupted Chris.

'No sign, according to the local team. The Helston station are dealing.'

'Why are you ringing us?' asked Greg, cutting to the chase.

'When we spoke before, you mentioned you were going further west. I wondered if you were anywhere near Helston. Look,' she said, a note of desperation in her voice, 'I'm worried about Debbie Lowson, and I'm afraid that more mistakes are being made. I've pushed my concerns as hard as I can, but I'm getting nowhere, other than a threat to my career. Inspector Challinor just isn't interested in Debbie as a priority. She says the father's death looks like natural causes, and if the daughter wasn't with him, that's a family matter not a crime. I don't think she wants to face the fact that her dislike of Kim Jones led to a mistake that is still having ramifications. So she's going through the motions of looking for Debbie Lowson, but half-heartedly. Whereas, I think what we have here is a sudden death and a woman gone to ground somewhere, who was quite possibly abused by her father and has recently given birth without medical attention.

'Frankly, it's a shitshow,' she burst out. 'And I don't know what you can do, but I thought if you were in the area you could perhaps ask around a bit at the least. Sorry,' she added. 'I'm not making much sense, am I? Sorry to mess up your holiday too.'

Greg had already turned the campervan off the A30 and towards Gwennap, Penryn and Helston.

'On our way,' said Chris into the phone. 'I'll ring you when we get there.'

Chris took over at the wheel for the last stint between Penryn and Helston on the grounds, as she put it, that they might meet more lanes as narrow as the eye of a needle. Greg gave way with good grace, aware that this gave him the chance to ring Sandy Tucker for an update.

'You can't believe how grateful I am,' were her opening words. 'I've been speaking to Helston, and they're concerned about Debbie Lowson too. Enough that they're organising a local search. This is on the basis that she seems to be vulnerable, rather than anything linked to the death of her father. They say that's enough justification for them.'

'When and where?' asked Greg.

'Helston. They're meeting volunteers at Flambards theme park. The park has apparently offered parking and other facilities,' she added. 'They plan to search between the town and the Loe as well as around the campervan site where the Lowsons' van was found.'

'The Loe?' asked Greg.

'It's a stretch of water inland from Loe Bar, the big shingle bank that cuts the Loe off from the sea.'

'OK. Got it.'

'I've mentioned to my friend at Helston that you're holidaying nearby.'

'Is the campsite still open? The one where Mr Lowson was found?'

'Yes. As it's not being treated as a suspicious death – currently.'

'OK. Then we'll go there and do a bit of chatting with the site owner and anyone else who seems helpful. If we come across your colleagues, should we mention your name?'

'Yes do,' said Sandy. 'Thank you, sir.'

'Greg,' said Greg automatically. 'Do call me Greg. And Sandy, don't get your hopes up. We'll look around and see if we can come up with any useful suggestions. But there's not much we can do really.'

'No, I know,' she said. 'But thank you. It makes me feel a bit better, knowing you're there.'

The campsite was small. The smallest they'd been on so far, with little space between the hardstandings for the motorhomes. The one at the far end of the site was half hidden behind a screen of bushes and festooned with police tape.

'Odd,' said Greg as Chris pulled up by the now closed and guarded main gate. 'I thought this wasn't a suspicious death.'

A uniformed constable came towards them as he spoke. His hair seemed chiselled rather than combed, and Greg, running a hand through his own slightly unkempt locks, wondered how the effect was achieved and whether it was worth it.

He introduced himself, 'Constable Trevelyan. 'Are you DCI Geldard and DS Mathews?'

'That's right,' said Greg through the open window. 'According to Sergeant Sandy Tucker the site was still open, and we were planning to stay here. But it seems things have moved on.'

'It's now being treated as a suspicious death, sir,' confirmed the young officer. 'But I've been told it's OK to let you in. If you'll just give me a second, I'll open the gate.'

Greg pushed the van door open and jumped down, going to help Constable Trevelyan with the gate.

'What's changed?' he asked. 'If you're allowed to tell me, that is.'

'I don't know a great deal,' said Trevelyan. 'Just that the doc isn't happy with the death and samples have gone for analysis. What samples and what analysis, I haven't a clue,' he said cheerfully. 'But Sandy Tucker said you'd had contact with the missing woman and might be able to help, so I was to let you in and let the search teams know you were here.'

7

The search

Chris parked in a bit of a hurry, and they did little more than leave their details with the site owner and plug the van into the electrical supply, for the benefit of the fridge, before walking over to the motorhome they recognised from their first stop in Cornwall.

A crime scene manager was standing by the tape, making notes on a tablet. Still clad in paper overalls, she had pushed the hood back. Her dark curly hair was sticking to her forehead and she was clearly struggling a little with the heat of the day. Just as she turned, with a question on her lips, Constable Trevelyan popped out from behind the motorhome and performed the introductions.

'Hannah, this is DCI Geldard and DS Mathews from Norfolk,' he said. 'They helped Sandy Tucker up-county.' Then turning to Greg, he added, 'This is Hannah Brakespear, the crime scene manager.'

'So it is being treated as a crime now, is it?' asked Greg once he had acknowledged the introduction.

'Seems so,' she replied, looking Greg over and clearly liking what she saw. Beside him, Greg could feel Chris bristle slightly and indulged himself with a hidden grin. 'For your ears only, sir, the doc thinks there's something dodgy about the death, and I was sent to look for potential toxins.'

'They think it was a poisoning?' asked Chris.

Hannah was perfectly polite, but her answer was mainly addressed to Greg. 'Her words were: *the cause of death was definitely heart failure, but that she could say that about most deaths*, and in this case she thought something had helped things along. I've got a few samples to take back to the lab.' She indicated the small pile of evidence bags at her feet. 'Mainly dried leaves from the store cupboard that I can't immediately identify, and some samples from the waste bin that might be of previous meals.'

'Do you know what raised her suspicions?' asked Greg.

'Something about inflammation in the gastric tract that looked unusual.'

Trevelyan had moved a few feet away to take a call on his radio. He turned to say, 'Sorry to interrupt, but if you want a word with the team organising the search, they'll be setting off shortly. I can give you a lift there, if you'd like.'

'Thank you, that would be great,' said Chris. 'Saves carting that monster down any more narrow lanes. Just need to pick up a couple of things and we'll be with you.'

'Meet you at the gate,' Trevelyan agreed.

By the time they'd picked up lightweight jackets and bottles of water from their campervan, the constable was waiting by the gate in a squad car. Greg got into the passenger seat at the front, and Chris into the back. If he was startled by the fluorescent orange, multi-pocketed waistcoat that Chris had donned, the constable kept his expression under stern control.

'Where are we going?' asked Greg.

'Down towards Loe Pool,' said Trevelyan. 'The area nearest the campsite has already been checked, and we've alerted everyone in town to check backyards, sheds and so on. That was when we thought we were looking for a vulnerable woman, rather than a suspected murderer, mind you.

'The only lead we've had, if it is a lead, was some discarded belongings at the side of the road that leads to Loe Pool. So that's where the search is focussed now. And as it's the largest natural lake in Cornwall, it presents us with a bit of a challenge. It's a nature reserve, but the ground around it is difficult to search and the water is very treacherous. Old-timers will tell you that Loe Pool takes a drowning every seven years,' he added.

'How long since the last one?' asked Chris.

'I'm not sure,' he said. 'Not since my time here, but a horse and rider got into difficulties not long ago, and said they were lucky to get out, so don't go into the water!'

'What was a horse doing in the water in the first place?' enquired Chris. 'Why would anyone ride into a dangerous lake?'

'Way I heard it,' said Trevelyan, 'the horse was being trained in dressage and had been taught to step sideways when the rider shifted her weight. Apparently, she forgot this important fact, leaned sideways to get under a low branch, and the horse did as it was told. Stepped sideways, straight into the water.'

Chris and Greg were still grinning when they met the officer in charge on the ground, a Sergeant Nicholl. He was more than happy to have more volunteers, and even happier that these two knew what they were doing.

'I've lots of locals who know the terrain, but few officers to keep an eye on them,' he said. 'The risk is, that if they do find anything, they compromise the evidence, but with a vulnerable woman out here somewhere, I can't afford to turn them away.'

'If you did, they'd probably just carry on anyway, without any guidance,' said Chris.

'Quite. So, if you would take charge of a group each, that would be brilliant.'

Greg's team was amongst the first to set off, as they had been designated the upper areas furthest from the lake. Chris couldn't help remarking, quietly to Greg, that his unfortunate history with the Norfolk Broads was obviously common knowledge across the whole country.

'Just you watch your step,' was his response. 'You're not known for caution around water either.' Then he followed his little band of three local teachers, a plumber and a fisherman over the uneven terrain to their starting point. He spaced them out in a line, far enough apart to cover as much ground as possible, but not so far that they missed something.

'And if you do find anything you think is unusual, don't touch it. Just give me a shout and wave an arm.' They nodded and set off slowly, all of them carrying sticks to help probe the thicker vegetation. It quickly got hot and steamy, and the myriad of irritating small flying things didn't help.

Two more fishermen, a holidaymaker on a break from the government agency Natural England, an amateur photographer and a stout barman from a pub in nearby Porthleven made up Chris's team. She went through much the same spiel as Greg had and they set off, straddling the path near the lake to cover its immediate shoreline and the ground close to the path. She was watching the barman with some concern as he puffed and blew near the lake, but he swiftly seemed to get a second wind. She had to ask him to slow down a bit, as he was getting ahead of the rest of the line.

After half an hour or so of finding nothing, she got a call from Sergeant Nicholl. 'Anything?' he asked.

'Not so far,' she replied. 'Can I ask you something? Are there any plans to get divers into the lake?'

'It's being debated,' said Nicholl. 'Thing is, there's a culvert used to pump water from the pool to prevent it backing up and flooding the lower parts of the town. It's dangerous to swim in the lake at any time, thanks to the thick weed on the bottom, but it's lethal if the pump is running. We need to make sure it's off before anyone goes into the water. And, between you and me, there seems to be someone dragging their feet about committing to the expense.'

As Chris rang off, the barman, who'd introduced himself as Barry, said, 'And of course, we don't want them finding Excalibur.'

'What?' asked Chris, fumbling to put her phone back in her rather over-tight pocket.

'Excalibur. King Arthur's sword. This is the lake it's supposed to have been thrown in by Sir Bedivere, after Arthur died.'

Chris looked round at the lake. 'It's a nice legend,' she said, and dropped her phone as she spoke. 'Damn!' she exclaimed. Then, 'Damn, damn and shit!'

It could have fallen onto one of the, admittedly few and far between, dry tussocks of grass. It hadn't. It had fallen into a deep puddle. She snatched it up, and tried to dry it off on her jeans.

'You need to get that home and put it into a bag of rice,' advised Barry. 'That's the best way to dry it out.'

Chris was pressing the screen and side buttons, but it did indeed seem to have died. 'Damn,' she said again, and this time put the phone in her small rucksack. *Nothing I can do with it just now.*

It was midday by the time they emerged onto Loe Bar. Chris felt quite at home, clambering over the enormous pile of flints. It was very reminiscent of a Norfolk beach after a storm. At the top, slightly out of breath, she was joined by Greg.

'Nothing!' they each confirmed to the other.

'Nicholl is thanking everyone and sending them home,' said Greg. 'At least we've ruled this area out. The search was pretty thorough, I think.'

'Except for the lake itself,' remarked Chris. 'I gather that's still being debated.'

'Apparently,' agreed Greg. 'Come on, let's get back to the road. We're promised a lift back to the campsite by Sergeant Nicholl.'

8

Later that day

That evening, tired from plodging around the lake and still scratching the multiple mosquito bites they had acquired, Greg and Chris had just curled up with a glass of wine each when a phone rang. Chris looked round automatically at the sound, then relaxed as she realised her phone was still buried in rice.

'Must be yours,' she said. 'Mine's still dead. Looks like I'm going to need a new one.'

Greg was thumbing the Home button on his phone as she spoke, then put it on speaker. 'It's Sandy,' he said.

'Hi, I gather from my mate Sid Nicholl that you helped out with the search today,' she said. 'I'm partly ringing to warn you that Inspector Challinor is on her way down, and to update you on the latest.'

'Taking an interest now, is she?' said Greg. 'What's triggered that?'

'The news that the hunt is probably for a killer, rather than a vulnerable woman. Yes, I know,' she added. 'She could be both. But I'm reflecting the inspector's comment, you understand.'

'It *was* poisoning then?' asked Chris.

'The analyses are back from both the post-mortem and the materials SOCO picked up in the motorhome. In fact, once the doc saw the samples, she made an educated guess and that's what speeded up the analyses. Like she says, it's always easier when you know what you're looking for.'

'Which was?' asked Greg

'Solanine and digitalis.'

'I know the second is a heart drug, but what's the first?' asked Greg.

'Green potatoes,' said Chris. 'It's why you don't eat green potatoes or feed them to livestock. They give you a nasty tummy upset at best. I didn't know it was lethal.'

'According to the doc, solanine poisoning isn't often lethal, but it does make you quite ill, as you said, and can cause neurological symptoms as well. Her theory is that the solanine was first used to make Mr Lowson ill, then when that didn't finish him off, foxgloves were added into the mix. Hence the original diagnosis of heart failure.'

'And that's what was found in the motorhome by Ms Brakespear?' asked Chris.

'There were the remains of a meal that had contained solanine in the bin, and the SOCO also found dried foxglove leaves in the cupboard.'

'Seems pretty conclusive,' observed Greg. 'Thanks for letting us know. In view of these developments and your inspector's imminent arrival, I think we'll return to minding our own business and our holiday.'

'Yes, I understand. Thanks for all your help,' said Sandy.

Chris looked at Greg as he put the phone down and picked up his glass of wine. 'Where next?' he asked. 'Back up towards St Ives, as we originally intended?'

'Now we're here, we might as well take a look around,' said Chris. 'There's always Penzance and St Michael's Mount. Lots to see in Falmouth too. Not to mention the Lost Gardens of Heligan. And the Eden Project.'

'Sounds like we'll have plenty to do to keep our minds off the Lowsons and their troubles,' said Greg. He returned Chris's gaze. 'I can tell from here that you don't like leaving it half finished. But it's not our job, and if we keep interfering, we're going to end up on the sharp end of a complaint. Or we'll get Sandy into trouble.'

'As far as a complaint is concerned, let her bring it on,' said Chris rebelliously, meaning her bête noire, Challinor. 'I'll complain her, if she tries it. But yes, I take your point about Sandy. Sadly, I think you're right. Nothing we can do now, even if Challinor is set to cock it all up again.'

'Let's head for Penzance tomorrow, and we might be able to get you a new phone there,' suggested Greg as a gust of wind shook their campervan. 'And if this weather deteriorates, we can head for the art galleries or something else indoors.'

'I suppose Penzance might have a phone shop,' said Chris dubiously. 'Otherwise, I'll have to wait until we're home. In the meantime, I've put my iPad on charge. I can at least get my emails on that, provided I can link to your phone because it's Wi-Fi only.'

'Sure, no problem,' said Greg. 'Provided I haven't run through my mobile data allowance.'

They had a quiet night except for the wind, and a relaxing morning, treating themselves to a wicked breakfast of pastries and coffee from a bakery in Helston.

'I like the look of their pasties as well,' said Chris, finishing up her coffee and Danish.

'Funny you should say that.' Greg indicated a slightly greasy bag beside him on the bench seat. 'I got a couple for our lunch.'

'Before we set off for Penzance, can I link to your phone and see if there's anything important waiting for me?'

'Sure.' Greg tapped on his phone to make his hot spot available while Chris did the necessary with her elderly iPad.

'Great,' she said. 'Somewhere on our travels today we should get enough signal for me to download my emails.' She parked her iPad in the seat pocket beside her and took the wheel. 'Shall we go?'

Thanks to her being occupied with driving, it was not until they parked in the short-stay car park at Marazion that she had chance to pick up the iPad and check her emails.

'Nothing very exciting here,' she said to Greg. 'Usual work stuff you'd have thought they could have kept until I get home, plus an update from Mum on how Tally's getting on. Not much else.'

She was about to put the tablet down, when she paused. 'Hang on,' she said. 'I'd forgotten I could pick up texts on here as well. I'll just check if any messages landed before my phone died...' She froze, looking down at the screen.

'Something bothering you?' asked Greg, his attention attracted by her sudden silence.

'There's a number I don't recognise, and the message is signed "Debbie",' she answered. 'I thought they said the Lowsons' phone was still in the motorhome and that Debbie didn't have one of her own.'

'Not that they knew of,' corrected Greg. 'Perhaps she has one she keeps quiet about. Or perhaps she's got hold of one since. The more interesting question is, how did she get your number?'

Chris looked faintly embarrassed. 'I gave her my card,' she said. 'Just in case she needed to talk to someone about her father. And that was before I knew he may have been sexually abusing her!'

'Before we get too excited,' added Greg, 'there is another possibility.'

'That this isn't Debbie Lowson at all. Yes, I'd thought of that,' said Chris. 'But I think there's a good chance it is. She's asking to talk to me.'

'You can't do that without talking to Cornwall police,' said Greg in the tone she knew meant *Don't argue with me, you know I'm right*. 'She's not just a vulnerable woman. She's now the prime suspect in a murder enquiry. At the very least, we now have a number they can use to locate her using phone-mast data. At best, we might be able to persuade her to turn herself in.'

'You mean *I* might be able to persuade her,' said Chris. 'OK. Let's contact Challinor and take it from there. But if she tries to push me out of this...' The threat was left unspoken.

9

Back in touch

The conversation with Challinor was frosty. It took some time to navigate various layers of civilian staff and junior officers before they made it as far as her own ears.

'It's worse than ringing the prime minister,' remarked Greg during one extended playing of dodgy electronic music over the vehicle's loudspeakers, his phone now, at last, paired with the campervan.

'When did you last ring the prime minister?' asked Chris, scepticism writ large on her face.

'Worse than I imagine it to be,' said Greg impatiently. 'Oh, come on, woman, you're an inspector not the Pope!' The phone crackled, the campervan shook in the ever-increasing wind, and a rather indignant voice demanded to know who she was speaking to.

'At last,' muttered Chris under her breath, not really caring whether she was audible or not.

'Inspector Challinor, this is Detective Chief Inspector Geldard. We have some intelligence about Debbie Lowson that we thought we should pass on.' Greg outlined the position swiftly, and there was a silence broken only by the whistle of the gale at the van windows.

'You've known this for how long?' asked Challinor.

'For' – Greg consulted his watch – 'two minutes before we attempted to speak to you. Any further delay since then has been due to your office procedures.'

'When was the message sent?'

'Just before 3pm yesterday.'

'That seems an unconscionable delay in picking it up,' was the icy response. Greg explained the accident to Chris's phone, as Chris could hardly bring herself to speak civilly. There was another silence.

'I assume you will be able to track the phone,' said Greg.

'Provided it's switched on, of course,' was the rejoinder. 'If we'd had this information last night, we might have been able to make some progress. As it is…' If a shrug could be audible, this one was. 'Thank you, Chief Inspector. We'll take it from here.' The call ended abruptly.

'Well bugger me with a stick of curried rhubarb,' exclaimed Chris. 'Not a thank you. Nothing. I'm sorry, Greg, but I'm not sitting on my hands any longer.' She seized her iPad and tapped crisply with her forefingers. Then put it down. 'Let's see what happens now!' she said.

'What have you done?' asked Greg with some foreboding.

'I've texted her to ask if she's all right and to suggest we meet. If she says no, nothing's changed. If she agrees, we've made a step forward.'

'And we'd have to share it with Challinor,' Greg pointed out.

'Of course. But maybe not straight away. Let's just wait and see, shall we?'

'Meantime, let's see if we can visit St Michael's Mount.'

They were thwarted in that desire too. The gale force winds, and rising seas meant the causeway to the island was closed and the ferry service suspended. After a visit to an exhibition of Troika pottery and an abortive hunt round town for a new iPhone for Chris, they headed back towards Helston. Their scheme was to drive on to Falmouth and then the Eden Project, but like plans of mice and men, it went agley.

'I've had a reply,' said Chris.

Greg was driving at the time. He shot a swift glance sideways to Chris bent over her iPad, then pulled off onto a lay-by. A sign up ahead pointed right to somewhere called Seworgan, he noted. As there were no buildings of any kind in sight, he assumed it was either a tiny village or a long way off.

'Tell me,' he said, trying but failing to hide the caution in his voice.

'She wants to meet me,' said Chris.

'Where?'

'She hasn't said yet.' Chris was tapping as she spoke.

'Don't tell me. You've said yes.'

'Of course I have.' Chris was impatient. 'What else would I say?'

What else? repeated Greg silently.

'She says head for Porthleven, and she'll text me a precise location this evening.'

Greg looked over his shoulder, assessed the road and decided that, if he was very careful, he could turn the campervan where the additional width of the lay-by made the task just a little easier. He started the manoeuvre while Chris texted her agreement to Debbie's proposal.

'And now, you have to tell Challinor,' said Greg.

Chris started to object. 'She'll do a runner if she spots lots of police cars.'

'So she will too if they start a search based on phone-mast pings,' said Greg. 'As they surely will anytime now. But they might hold off the blue lights until this evening if there's a promise of a more precise location.'

Chris scowled her agreement. 'But you can make the call,' she stipulated. 'I'm not talking to that woman.'

This time Greg short-circuited the many layers of officialdom and rang Sergeant Sid Nicholl.

'I'll pass it on, thank you, sir,' he said. 'If Inspector Challinor wants to speak to you, should she use this number?'

'Yes,' said Greg, and went back to concentrating on his driving. By 6pm they were parked on a site above the harbour town of Porthleven, a short distance from a pub overlooking the harbour.

10

Porthleven

'Now what?' asked Chris, checking her messages roughly every fifteen seconds. 'Should I message again?'

'No,' advised Greg. 'You risk spooking her. Either she'll do as she said, or she won't. You chasing her is more likely to provoke the latter.'

Chris acknowledged the sense of his advice, but she was temperamentally unsuited to waiting patiently. Greg spotted the signs as, indeed, a deaf, blind, sleeping sloth would have been bound to do.

'Come on,' he said, rising and grabbing his puffa jacket. 'Let's go to the pub. We can at least have a drink and a snack while we're waiting.' Muttering, Chris grabbed her coat too, tucked her iPad into the shelter of its poacher's pocket and followed Greg out into the increasingly wild weather battering the clifftop. They made their way to the pub, fighting to avoid being blown along like flotsam as the onshore wind pushed them ahead of it down the narrow lane to the Fishermen's Arms.

While Greg went to the bar, Chris seized the opportunity, offered by a couple of departing customers, to grab a table in the window. Although bursts of rain spattered the glass with growing strength, it still afforded a spectacular view of the harbour. With the wind in this direction, blowing straight into the mouth of the narrow bay, the breakers surged down to hammer with spectacular force into the wall that protected the inner harbour. Even there, as Chris noted, craning her neck, the water was distinctly choppy and the colourful boats of the fishing fleet were bobbing like corks.

Shaking some of the rain off her coat, she hung it on the back of her chair and checked her iPad for messages. Again, nothing. Greg came back with a couple of pints and his pockets stuffed variously with packets of crisps, peanuts and pork scratchings.

'I thought these would keep us going for now,' he said. 'But if she doesn't contact you, it's not all bad news. This place has a good menu. We could have supper here and then spend the night where we're parked, just up the road. Oh, and your mate Barry says "Hi".'

Chris looked over at the bar and recognised the man from the search by the Loe. She waved an acknowledgement and turned back to Greg. 'This has been a rather odd holiday, hasn't it?' she said.

'Not our fault,' said Greg, ripping open a packet of crisps. 'And I do share your concern for Debbie Lowson. I'm just rather more worried than you about treading on local toes.'

'Even though they're incompetent?' challenged Chris.

'Well, there is that,' admitted Greg.

They had consumed all their salty snacks before Chris exclaimed, rather loudly, 'Yes!' and punched the air. Several locals propping up the bar turned in surprise, then shrugged and turned back again. *No accounting for grockles!*

'She's suggesting ten minutes from now, down by the harbour,' said Chris.

'Which side? We'll struggle to get round the end and over to the other side in ten minutes,' exclaimed Greg.

'This side, where the harbour wall divides the inner harbour from the outer,' said Chris.

'I think she's seen our campervan and knows we'll be somewhere round here. She may even know we're in the pub. And she's given us a tight deadline to avoid other people joining the party. It's what I'd do,' she said.

'She's not stupid,' agreed Greg. 'Come on, we'd better get a shift on.' He was pulling his coat on as he spoke. 'I'll ring Nicholl as we walk down the hill. It's up to him then.'

Outside, it was immediately obvious the wind had strengthened. Huge breakers were now crashing over the harbour wall, and they had to shout to make themselves heard. Down where the outer and inner harbour were divided, as specified by Debbie, they found themselves a slightly more sheltered corner by a white-painted cottage and lurked there.

'Did you ring them?' asked Chris.

'Yes. I spoke to Nicholl,' said Greg. He might have said more, but they were startled by a sudden appearance around the corner of the cottage. On a calmer night, they would have heard her approaching footsteps. As it was, the first intimation they had of Debbie's presence was the silhouette of a bulky jacket and sodden hair appearing in front of them.

'Just you,' she said, pointing at Chris. 'Not him. I guessed he'd be here, but I'm not talking to him.'

Greg nodded his understanding. 'On condition you stay within sight of me,' he said.

Debbie hesitated, then nodded her agreement and led Chris across the road to stand by the stone wall, near where the cliff fell down into the boiling sea below. Beyond the shelter of the cottage, the wind whipped both women's hair around their faces. Greg watched as Chris scooped hers back with one hand and waved the other urgently to reinforce whatever point she was making. He assumed she was attempting to reassure Debbie and persuade her to turn herself in.

That was, indeed, exactly the thrust of Chris's argument. She started by asking how Debbie was and expressing concern that she'd had no medical attention since giving birth.

Debbie, in tacit admission that she was indeed the mother, had said she was feeling better now. 'You do understand,' she said urgently. 'I had to do it.' Then she dropped her voice, and whatever she said was carried away on the wind.

'Sorry, I didn't catch that,' half shouted Chris.

'I said, my baby was dead. She never breathed. I didn't kill her. I wouldn't kill her, even though...'

'Even though she was the product of rape?' asked Chris, deciding that brutal honesty was her best bet at this point.

'You know that?' asked Debbie. 'How do you know that? I never told anyone. Not after my mother wouldn't believe me.'

'Your father assaulted you even before your mother died?' asked Chris, wishing above all else that this was a conversation in a quiet room rather than on a street in a gale.

'She was ill. But I'm sure she knew – even though she wouldn't believe me. How do you know?' asked Debbie again.

'DNA from the placenta,' said Chris. 'It showed your father was also the baby's father.'

'Oh.' It was a long, drawn-out sigh. 'I thought no one would believe me. I thought no one would understand why...'

Again, Chris lost the end of the sentence. She took a guess at what she had missed.

'Why you killed your father?' she asked. She put her head close to Debbie's and an arm around her shoulders. 'Was that it, Debbie?'

On the other side of the street, Greg, watching, heaved a sigh of relief. It looked as though Chris was getting through to her.

'There was no other way to stop him,' said Debbie. 'I couldn't risk another dead baby. It was evil, what he did to me. And more babies would die.'

Chris tightened her arm around the shaking shoulders. 'More babies?' she asked. 'Had it happened before?'

There was a moment while the noises of the wind and the sea took over, and Chris scraped her wet hair back from her face again with her spare hand. Debbie put her mouth close to Chris's ear and said, 'I'd already had a miscarriage. At least one. Perhaps two. His babies were doomed. I had to stop him.'

'If you'll come with me to the police station, I can help you explain,' Chris said. 'I'm sure they'll understand.'

'I'll have to go to prison, won't I?' said Debbie.

'Probably,' said Chris honestly. 'But not necessarily. It all depends—'

She was interrupted by blue flashing lights approaching from the street above and a second set from the direction of the town centre. The blue lights reflected eerily in fragments from the white tops of the crashing breakers.

'This is a trap,' shouted Debbie as she spun from the protecting arm and dashed away in the only direction open to her, along the harbour wall.

Greg, not entirely surprised by the blue lights, was quickly on her tail, barrelling past Chris and knocking her to the side with his shoulder. Chris clung to the rain-soaked wall to catch her balance, and she shouted a warning. Then she set off after Greg.

Even the landward edge of the sea wall was flooded with seawater, and the breakneck pace of, first Debbie, then Greg, slowed as they both slithered and slipped. The tail end of waves breaking clean over the wall hit them around knee height, making them stagger. Debbie went flying to the inner edge of the breakwater and ended up leaning on the upper wall. Greg also lurched to the side but managed to keep his feet, now gaining on the woman ahead of him.

'Debbie! Debbie!' he shouted. 'Come back. Chris and I will look after you.'

She either didn't hear or ignored him, and pushing herself off the wall headed further out towards the end of the breakwater. As they both left the slight shelter afforded by the cliff above them, the wind's note rose to a scream and the height of the waves breaking across the wall rose from knee height to shoulder, to...

Greg hesitated for a fraction of a second. Chris grabbed for his arm and missed just as he lunged forward and got a grip on the back of Debbie Lowson's shiny, black puffa jacket. For a long moment they teetered on the edge of the sea wall, then the jacket, made slick by rain and seawater, slipped through Greg's desperately clutching fingers. The next huge wave took Debbie Lowson and toppled her over into the troubled waters of the inner harbour.

Greg also lurched to the wall, caught in the same powerful surge of icy water and, for a moment that took Chris's breath away, seemed to hover on the edge of going over. Chris reached out again just as the backwash pulled Greg back from the brink, their fingers caught, slipped, then caught again in a desperate grip.

11

Conclusions

For a long moment Chris and Greg stood, lashed by wind, waves and disbelief. Then they turned and with difficulty made their way back towards the cliff-edge road and the growing accumulation of blue flashing lights.

The first officer they recognised was Nicholl. 'Lowson?' he asked.

'Gone,' said Greg, his arm round a stunned Chris.

Inspector Challinor bustled up behind Nicholl, the crackling of her waterproofs audible even over the storm.

'I need you to come to the station with us,' she said.

'Of course,' said Greg. 'After we've changed and dried off...'

'Now,' said Challinor.

Greg regarded her for a moment, in silence. Even the storm seemed to fade a little and Chris held her breath. She had never seen Greg look so angry. Challinor opened her mouth again, and then shut it.

'I don't think you can have heard me correctly,' said Greg, in a voice so cold Chris half expected the water around them to freeze. 'I have said that we will come to whatever station you wish to make our statements, after we have dried ourselves and changed. Not before. And if I were you, I wouldn't be in any hurry to hear what I have to say about the conduct of this investigation.'

There was another pause, then Challinor said stiffly, 'I'll expect you within the hour. I think we'll deal with this at Truro.'

'We'll deal with this at Truro, *sir*,' prompted Greg.

'Sir.' Challinor forced the word through stiff lips and turned away.

Nicholl stepped forward. 'I'll run you back to your campervan,' he offered.

Greg nodded, and gave Chris a little push towards the car. 'Thank you, Sergeant,' he said.

There was a silence in the car for the duration of the short journey back to the clifftop, where the campervan was shuddering under the wind's hammer blows.

Nicholl pulled up alongside and turned to his two backseat passengers. 'I can wait, and you can follow me to Truro, if you like,' he offered. 'Or I can drive you there. Or you make your own way. Whichever you prefer.'

Greg looked at Chris, and an unspoken agreement passed between them. 'We'll accept a lift, thank you, Sergeant,' said Greg. 'It's been a long night already, and I don't think either of us wants to drive that thing anywhere in this wind.'

He nodded to the campervan. 'Give us a few minutes to change, and we'll be with you.'

It took them only moments to strip off the wet things and dry themselves on towels, hampered only slightly by the lack of space. Greg dressed swiftly in dark trousers, white shirt and the only dry jacket he now had, a navy fleece. Chris pulled on dark jeans and a black top, and having wiped the worst of the wet off her bright yellow oilskins, put them back on. Her wet hair was twisted into a knot at the back of her head and she looked both professional and purposeful.

'What are you going to say?' she asked Greg.

'The truth,' he said shortly. 'That this investigation was unprofessional from the start and resulted in the death of a vulnerable suspect.'

'You know that will probably get us into trouble,' said Chris. 'I get the impression Challinor has friends in high places. How else does she get away with behaving the way she did with Kate Jones?'

'So, we might have a bit of rough ground to get over, but I doubt her reach extends to the IOPC,' said Greg. 'Come on, let's get it over with. A bit of hassle's never bothered us in the past.'

Chris leaned forward. 'I love you, Detective Chief Inspector,' she said. 'And never more than when you're on a crusade. Come on. Let's go get 'em.'

The drive to Truro was also conducted mostly in silence, only this time Greg sat in the passenger seat beside Nicholl, leaving Chris in the back, checking times and dates, and making notes on her iPad.

Nicholl cleared his throat a couple of times as though preparing to speak, but it wasn't until the outskirts of Truro that he managed to articulate his apology.

'Sorry about the "all lights blazing" approach,' he said. 'It wasn't my choice. I recommended low-key, like you said when we spoke.'

Greg didn't take his eyes off the road ahead. 'So I imagined,' he said. 'But thank you for the confirmation.'

'May I say something else, sir?' said Nicholl, then carried on without waiting for permission. 'Sandy told me what happened up-country. About the teenager, I mean. Did you know Inspector Challinor is a single mother?'

'No. And that is relevant why?' enquired Greg.

'Rumour has it that the chief constable is her son's father.'

'I don't like gossip, Sergeant,' said Greg.

No, but I do, thought Chris and leaned forward to hear better.

'Just saying, she has friends in high places,' said Nicholl, and shut up, much to Chris's regret.

That they were expected at the police station was evidenced by the swiftness with which they were whisked through the reception area, down a long corridor and into the interview suite. There they settled themselves at the usual, slightly battered, table and awaited developments.

'She surely isn't planning on interviewing us under caution,' muttered Chris to Greg, one eye on the two-way mirror.

Totally confident that Inspector Challinor was observing them from the next room, Greg said clearly, 'I'm sure she wouldn't be so stupid. We're just here to make our statements, out of *professional* courtesy.' He added loudly, 'I like my coffee black, no sugar. Sergeant Mathews would like a tea with milk and one sugar.' Then he leaned back with just the faintest grin.

The hot drinks materialised in the hands of a uniformed constable shortly after. He put them down on the table, added some wrapped biscuits from his pocket then said, 'I'll bring you some paper and pens, sir, and Sarge. Inspector Challinor will be with you shortly.'

The inspector arrived at the same time as the writing materials. 'I appreciate you are familiar with the procedures,' she said. 'I would just like to make it clear that we need to know precisely how the suspect and you came to be on the harbour wall, and what precipitated her dash onto the breakwater. I'm not sure whether this qualifies as a death in police custody, as you are not on the Cornwall force. But I have, in any event, referred the matter to the IOPC, and they will probably wish to investigate.'

'I will be happy to cooperate with any such investigation,' said Greg. 'And I'm sure that its terms will be drawn sufficiently widely to encompass *all* the factors which contributed to the tragic outcome earlier tonight.' Challinor flushed and withdrew.

Chris looked at Greg and glanced at the mirror again. 'So that's how she's playing it,' she said softly. 'Blaming us.'

'Predictable and futile,' said Greg calmly. 'Come on. Let's get this finished and get on our way.'

Sipping coffee and tea respectively, they wrote. Chris finished first and leaned back. 'I'd kill for another cuppa,' she said.

By the time Greg put his pen down, the coffee and tea had arrived in the hands of the same grinning constable. 'Sergeant Nicholl said to ask you if you'd like a bacon sarnie each,' he said.

'Thank you, that would be great,' said Chris.

When he returned with the specified bacon sandwiches, they swopped manuscripts and read in silence for a while, trying, with limited success, to keep grease and crumbs off the paperwork.

'I like this bit,' said Chris looking up, and read aloud from Greg's statement.

' "To summarise, the initial investigation into the death of the baby was fatally flawed by the unevidenced assumption that the site manager's daughter was involved. This led to a failure to explore other avenues of enquiry and the premature release of what was, at the least, a key witness and could justifiably have been regarded as a prime suspect.

' "The subsequent deaths of both Mr Lowson and his daughter could have been prevented if a more open and dispassionate mind had addressed the existing evidence and particularly the results of the analysis of the infant's DNA."

'And this bit. "It is acknowledged to be unfortunate that the damage to Sergeant Mathews's iPhone during the volunteer search for Ms Lowson led to a delay in receipt of a key communication. However, all intelligence derived from Sergeant Mathews's contact with the suspect was immediately passed to the relevant authority.

' "Finally, I find it deeply regrettable that my advice to approach the suspect discreetly and with care was ignored, and that the consequent approach by a mob of police cars with flashing blue lights precipitated the flight and subsequent death of a vulnerable woman."

'However, I'm not sure "mob" would be termed professional language,' she added.

'It stands,' said Greg firmly. 'Come on, let's get copies to take with us, and get on our way.'

In the corridor they were intercepted by an Inspector Challinor who was so flushed as to appear purple.

'I'll take those,' she said.

'Not yet,' said Greg. 'We will take copies for our own reference first. And you'll find we have included our contact details so that the IOPC can contact us for any clarification required.' He marched ahead of her to the open-plan office they had passed on their way to the interview suite and pushed the door open, Challinor trotting ineffectually in his wake. He ignored her squawking and raised his voice to ask, ' Could anyone copy these for me?'

'Certainly, sir,' said Sergeant Nicholl, leaping to his feet. 'Won't take a moment.'

Outside in the fresh air again, Greg and Chris both took deep breaths and looked around them. 'I wonder where the nearest taxi rank is,' said Chris, 'since we haven't been offered a lift back to Porthleven.'

'That wasn't ever going to happen, was it,' said Greg with a grin. 'Come on, let's wander down towards the cathedral.' As they turned away, a taxi drew up beside them.

The driver leaned over and shouted through the open passenger window, 'Chief Inspector Geldard and Sergeant Mathews? I gather you need a ride to Porthleven?'

'Yes, how did you...'

'Sergeant Nicholl booked me for you,' he said. 'Hop in.'

12

Postscript

Three days later, in the aftermath of the storms, fisherman Joe Hawkins sculled across Porthleven's inner harbour to his crabber, the *Emily Anne*, to check for damage and ready her for sea. He was concerned to note that she was listing slightly to starboard, and rowed around her to see if he could identify any obvious damage. As he rounded the prow, he looked along the length of his boat and spotted something caught up on the line to the buoy. A couple of strokes of his oar brought him close enough to identify it, and one more pull turned his dinghy for the shore and a phone call to the coastguard.

Sergeant Nicholl was amongst the police officers who answered the call from the coastguard. As the Lizard lifeboat was already responding to a shout, the police engaged assistance from Joe and a couple of his friends to transport the forensic team to the body floating alongside the *Emily Anne*. In due course, as the bagged body came up the slipway and was loaded into the unmarked hearse, Nicholl dialled a number he'd saved to his phone.

'Geldard,' said a brisk voice.

'I thought you'd like to know, sir, Debbie Lowson's body has been found in the harbour, here in Porthleven.'

There was a silence. 'Poor woman,' said Greg. 'I knew once she went over that wall, she had no chance. Such a waste.'

'Yes, sir,' said Nicholl. 'I thought you might also like to know that the case has been referred to the IOPC.'

'Yes, I knew that, thank you. They have been in touch. And thank you for letting me know about Debbie Lowson. I'll pass it on to Sergeant Mathews.'

'It was good to meet you, sir, and thank you,' said Nicholl. And rang off.

Greg looked across his desk to Chris.

'Debbie,' she said. It wasn't a question.

'When we go on holiday next year,' said Greg, 'how do you feel about Iceland? Surely we can't get into any trouble there.'

Printed in Dunstable, United Kingdom

63410794R10058